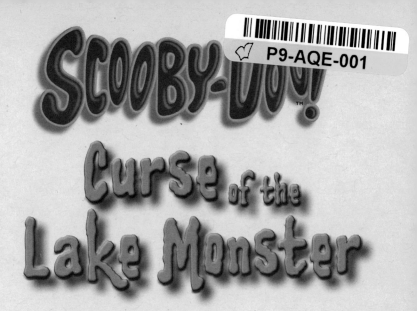

SCOOBY-DOO!

Curse of the Lake Monster

Adapted by
Laura Dower

Based upon the film written by
Steven Altiere & Daniel Altiere

Based on characters created by
Hanna-Barbera Productions

SCHOLASTIC INC.
New York   Toronto   London   Auckland
Sydney   Mexico City   New Delhi   Hong Kong

ISBN 978-0-545-28665-7

12 11 10 9 8 7 6 5 4 3 2 1   10 11 12 13 14 15/0

Printed in the U.S.A.   40

First printing, October 2010

CHAPTER

Shaggy glared at the wall clock inside Spanish class.

Tick . . . tick . . . tick . . .

In just a few short minutes, he and his pals would be running to grab their surfboards.

Tick . . . tick . . .

HEY!

All at once, the hands on the clock ticked *backward.*

"Like . . . that's moving in the wrong direction!" Shaggy exclaimed.

Thankfully, a split second later, the clock hands ticked forward.

Brrrrrrrrrrrrring.

The school bell chimed loudly, and students all over the school building let out a scream. Now school really *was* out for summer!

Shaggy dashed into the hall with the other students. Was that confetti and balloons raining down from the ceiling?

"Good times!" Shaggy cried. He raced for the front door. Everywhere he looked, kids bounced beach balls and twirled around like hula dancers. And right there in the middle of it all was Scooby-Doo and his conga drum.

"SHAGGY!" Velma whistled. She stood at the bottom of the school steps.

Shaggy stopped short when he saw her.

"Huh? Like, Velma, can't you see I'm ready to catch a wave?"

"Quit daydreaming, Shag," Velma said. "I know you're excited. But right now we have places to go. Our seasonal employment awaits! Fred and Daphne said they'd meet us in the parking lot."

Shaggy blinked hard. "Daydreaming? But—"

He glanced behind him. Students who had been decked out in bathing trunks and Polynesian hula skirts moments before were now wearing ordinary school clothes. There wasn't a beach ball in sight. Scooby was there, but he didn't have any drum.

Brrrrrrrrrrrrrring.

"Hurry up!" Velma said. "We have to go now!"

Shaggy pulled off his sneaker and tipped it

upside-down. Sand poured out onto the ground.

"Daydreaming, huh?" Shaggy said. "Like, I didn't even have time to get a tan!"

"Ruh-roh!" Scooby giggled. "Retter ruck rext time!"

Velma hurried across the parking lot. Shaggy and Scooby raced after her.

"Sure is lucky that Daphne's uncle is opening his new country club this summer, right, V?" Shaggy said.

"Indeed!" Velma said. "Without summer jobs at his club, we'd never be able to pay back Old Man Frickert for the damage we did to his barn."

Shaggy nodded. "You mean the damage *I* did. . . ."

"Yeah, we almost solved the case of the Vengeful Scarecrow," Velma said. She put her hands on her hips and frowned. "But you got a little too fired up about that one, didn't you, Shag?"

"Hey!" Shaggy shrugged. "Just for the record, nowhere on those bales of hay did it say flammable. . . ."

Velma sighed. "Tell that to Old Man Frickert. That barn burner cost us big time. Remember what he said?"

Shaggy nodded. He made a face and put on an accent like Old Man Frickert. "Unless you can come up with ten thousand dollars to rebuild my barn," Shaggy croaked, "the only mystery around here will be how you meddling kids can stay out of jail!"

At last, Velma, Shaggy, and Scooby arrived at the Mystery Machine. It was parked under a big tree.

"Where are Daphne and Fred?" Velma asked, checking her watch. "Daphne said we should get on the road right after school."

Shaggy pulled the back door of the van wide open.

"Like, *whoa*!" he cried.

"DAPHNE? FRED? What are you doing?" Velma said.

From inside the back seat, Daphne and Fred broke apart. They had been *kissing*!

Scooby covered his eyes with his big paws.

"Like, what was *that* about?" Shaggy asked, shocked.

Daphne smoothed down her hair. "What was *what*?" she stammered.

"I think we need an explanation," Shaggy said. "I know what I just saw and . . ."

"Ree, too!" Scooby seconded.

"Hmmm," Velma murmured. "There's always been an undeniable chemistry between the two of you. When did the transformative reaction finally occur?"

"Well . . ." Fred said sheepishly. "I guess it sort

of started in Old Man Frickert's barn."

"Remember, Velma?" Daphne said. "We followed the trail of the Vengeful Scarecrow up into the hayloft. . . ."

"*Roworroooo!*" Scooby giggled. "Rurn, raby, rurn!"

"I guess you could say we had this 'hayloft moment,'" Daphne explained.

"Hmmm, well," said Velma, "although your crush is sweet, I feel obligated to raise one concern. Whenever there's a shift in the relationship between two individuals within a group, it inevitably has repercussions on the group as a whole, so . . ."

"Oh," said Daphne, blushing. "You're embarrassing me."

"Don't worry, Daph," Shaggy said. "Like, we're all way too mature to let anything change the way we act in the Mystery Machine. Right, Scoob?"

"Ray roo rature!" Scooby barked.

Fred started up the engine. As the car revved forward, Scooby gave Shaggy a double-knuckle punch.

"Runchbuggy rellow!" Scooby yelped. He pointed to a yellow car that was passing by.

"Punchbuggy blue!" Shaggy cried back, punching his friend on the leg. Then he punched

Scooby again. "PUNCHBUGGY GREEN!"

Before long, the two were wrestling in the back. "*ROOOWOOWOOOROOOO!*"

"Oh, yeah, *that's* mature," Daphne said, rolling her eyes.

* * *

The Mystery Machine logged a lot of miles that day. The gang passed buildings, trees, farms, schools, and forests.

"You do know where we're headed, right?" Velma asked Fred after a few hours.

"Don't worry. We're not lost," Fred said.

He turned the Mystery Machine down a rocky road. The sign at the side of the road read WELCOME TO ERIE POINTE.

The road led them into a quaint fishing village. There was, however, no sign of their final destination.

"Like, where's the country club?" Shaggy asked. "My tummy's rum-rum-rumbling."

"Ree, roo!" Scooby said. "Rooby racktime!"

"There has to be someone in this town who can give us directions," Daphne said.

"This is a *town*?" Fred gulped. "Looks like a bunch of boats to me."

The marina was filled with empty, deserted

fishing boats. One boat was up on risers. Someone had painted it a deep shade of purple.

Shaggy pointed out the window. "Look!" he said. "It's the S.S. Daphne!"

Everyone laughed. "Very funny," Daphne said, admiring her purple dress. It was her favorite color.

"Hey," Velma said. "There's a general store. Let's check it out."

"Trowburg's Gas and Goods," Daphne said, reading the store sign.

The Mystery Machine pulled in and the gang hopped out. A screen door creaked in the wind. An old ice chest wheezed open and then shut.

Clang!

"Hello?" Fred called out. "Anyone here?"

Shaggy and Scooby noticed a picture high on the wall. It showed a creepy woman with stringy hair and a scowl.

HILDA TROWBURG, PROPRIETOR.

"Like, zoinks!" Shaggy said. "Let's ditch this Popsicle stand and find the country club. . . ."

"COUNTRY CLUB!?" a voice howled from behind the group.

Everyone turned around and gasped.

It was Hilda Trowburg. And she looked even meaner than her picture.

CHAPTER

2

"**Z**oinks!" Shaggy cried. "Like, where in the middle of nowhere did *you* come from?"

"Stay away from the country club!" Hilda Trowburg said. "You must turn back while you still can."

"Huh?" Velma said. "But we just got here!" She turned and began to flip through a stack of brochures on a table by the cash register.

"Excuse me, ma'am, but why would we want to leave?" Fred asked Hilda.

"We have summer jobs at the country club," Daphne said.

"Country club? Don't say it!" Hilda howled. Her eyes flashed and her face turned beet red. Scooby was shaking in his fur at the sight of this spooky shop owner.

Hilda's voice got very low. "I told them not to

build out there. I tried to warn them. I told them the monster would return. But they just thought I was a crazy old hag."

"H-h-hag? You?" Shaggy gulped. "Nah, not you . . ."

"Mark my words!" Hilda yelled. "The Lake Monster will return! And you will all be sorry!"

Daphne gulped. Hilda Trowburg made her very nervous. "Uh, guys . . . maybe we should—"

"Ret rout of here?" Scooby yowled.

"You heard the lady!" Shaggy said.

Without missing a beat, Shaggy and Scooby flew through the door of Trowburg's Gas and Goods. They were followed by Daphne and Fred. Velma ran out, too, with her stack of brochures. They raced for the Mystery Machine.

"Where now?" Fred started the engine. "That lady gave me a case of the creeps."

"Oh, drat! We ran out of there so fast we didn't get directions to the club!" Daphne said.

"I know the right directions," Shaggy yelped. "Like, make a U-turn and head anywhere but here!"

"But that'll take us right back to Coolsville," Fred said.

"Yeah, well, sourpuss back there said there's a monster in the lake! And, like, that's one monster I don't *ever* want to meet," Shaggy said.

"Hold on," Velma said. "Did you say *monster*?"

"Like, weren't you listening? That crazy hag in there just said there was a—"

"RONSTER!" Scooby barked.

"Was she talking about *this* monster?" Velma held up a brochure she'd been reading. On the front of the brochure were the words VISITOR'S GUIDE TO ERIE POINTE. Velma turned to a page with a great big, blurry photograph. It was a photo of a shady-looking monster. And it was standing on the bank of a lake. *This* lake! Erie Lake!

"It says here," Velma read, "that for hundreds of years, there have been sightings of a hideous creature said to live at the bottom of Erie Lake."

"Oh!" Fred rolled his eyes. "So there isn't an actual monster. This is just one of those things like Bigfoot or Loch Ness."

"BIGFOOT?!" Shaggy cried. "Zoinks! This is worse than I thought!"

"No, Shaggy," Daphne said. "What Fred is saying is that the Lake Monster is probably nothing more than a tall tale or a legend, like Bigfoot. Lots of small towns make up legends. That way, people come from miles around to visit the place!"

"Oh, sure," Shaggy said. "Like, come for the scenery . . . stay for certain death!"

"Rertain reath?" Scooby jumped right into Shaggy's arms. *"Rwoooowrrooo!"*

"Come on, you two, quit the scaredy-cat attack," Fred said. "We have to go or we'll be late to meet Uncle Thorny at the country club. Let's stick to the original plan."

Velma opened another brochure with a small map. "This should help us get there," she said, pointing. It was marked ERIE POINTE COUNTRY CLUB.

* * *

Just like that, the gang was off in search of the country club's front gates.

According to the map, the club was just a short distance from Trowburg's. Velma kept track of the mileage. She was good with numbers.

Shaggy and Scooby huddled together in the back seat. They didn't even want to peek out of the window. After all, what if the monster popped up in their path? Better not to look at all.

It only took a few minutes to reach a massive pair of metal gates with an engraved sign that read ERIE POINTE COUNTRY CLUB.

"Aha!" Fred said as he turned into the long, winding drive.

The Mystery Machine drove a short way before passing a small clubhouse near the lake. The golf course here was grand: a mix of lush, emerald-colored fairways and greens dotted with sand traps. A lawn maintenance crew was rushing around, getting things in shipshape order.

"Rancy shmancy!" Scooby said, peeking out the window.

"You said it, Scoob!" Shaggy agreed.

"This *is* pretty swank, Daph," Fred added. "Your uncle Thorny outdid himself this time."

Fred pulled over and parked the van. Daphne hopped out just in time to see a distinguished-looking gentleman appear on one of the wide green lawns. He was dressed in a designer suit, and his cufflinks sparkled in the sun.

"Uncle Thorny!" Daphne cried.

"Daphne!" Uncle Thorny replied, hurrying over.

"Gang," said Daphne, "meet Thornton Blake IV, otherwise known as my uncle Thorny. Uncle Thorny, this is the gang: Fred, Velma, Shaggy . . ."

"And Rooby-Rooby-Roo!" Scooby yowled. "Rice to reet you."

Uncle Thorny laughed and shook Scooby's paw. Scooby couldn't resist the photo-op. He threw his arm around Thorny and pulled

Daphne's uncle in for a close-up. Shaggy sidled right up, too.

"Like, thanks a zillion, Uncle T, for havin' us," Shaggy said. "Looks like you've got a real swinging club here. Ha, ha! Get it? Swinging? Club?"

He pretended to tee off with an imaginary golf club.

Uncle Thorny grinned. "Yup, I've got high hopes for this place, Shaggy. But I'm going to need your help. *Lots* of help."

"Ready when you are, Uncle!" Daphne said.

"Daphne and Velma, I've given you waitstaff duties in the clubhouse café. Fred and Shaggy, I've assigned you to the links as golf caddies. Scooby, you can help out, too. Sound good?"

"Rabsorutely!" Scooby said.

Uncle Thorny showed everyone to the staff quarters in the main house. Then he reminded them to get a good night's sleep.

"We start our shifts at six A.M. sharp!" Thorny said before disappearing up a flight of stairs. "Catch some Zs, kids!"

"Like, I'll get the luggage," Shaggy volunteered.

Without missing a beat, he hopped up on the back of the Mystery Machine to grab the bags. But just as he hoisted a heavy suitcase into the air, Shaggy lost his balance.

He was about to crash on the ground. But lucky for him, Velma was right there! She reached out and caught Shaggy in midair.

"Jinkies, that was close. Are you all right?" Velma asked, cradling him in her arms.

Shaggy shook his head. "Huh?" He blinked at Velma. Behind her head, a golden orange sunset cast a romantic glow. For a split second, Velma looked . . . well, dreamy.

Shaggy looked at Velma. Velma looked at Shaggy.

"Uh, Shag," Velma said.

"*Yeeees . . .*" Shaggy said in a sweet-as-sugar voice.

"Shag, I don't think I can . . ."

"*Yeeees . . .*"

"Hold you much longer!" Velma cried.

And just like that, she dropped Shaggy onto the ground with a loud thud.

Not that Shaggy noticed the fall, or anything else. All he saw was a groovy golden sunset and the thousand-watt smile on Velma Dinkley's face.

CHAPTER

After everyone got settled into their rooms, Shaggy pulled Scooby aside. He needed to talk.

"Like, can I tell you a secret?" Shaggy asked his four-legged friend.

"Rah! Rah!" Scooby said, panting.

"Scoob, I think that I may have had a hayloft moment," Shaggy said. "Like Daphne and Fred. *A hayloft moment.*"

Scooby gave Shaggy a blank stare. "Mmmmhuh?"

"Scoob, do you think it's possible that . . . Velma and I are meant to be?"

"Rou and Rhelma!?" Scooby asked. He stepped back with a thoughtful look on his face. Then he fell to the ground laughing hysterically!

"Gee," Shaggy said. "Thanks for the support,

Scoob. I'll remember this come flea season."

"Reriously?" Scooby said, starting to itch. "Ruh-roh!"

After that, the gang settled in for the night. It was going to be a busy morning and everyone needed his or her beauty sleep.

* * *

At the crack of dawn, the kids headed straight for the Erie Pointe Golf Course. As they ambled along, Shaggy quietly took the opportunity to ask Fred a few important questions about dating — just in case the information came in handy.

"How do you go from girl who is your friend to *girlfriend*?" Shaggy asked Fred.

"Why are you asking me that?" Fred shrugged.

"Well, you and Daphne, of course. . . ."

"Daphne!? She's not my girlfriend!" Fred exclaimed. "We're just . . . er . . . hanging out. I'm not a relationship kind of guy. I'm a football player, remember? We like to play the field. . . ."

"Whatever you say, man," Shaggy said, feeling a little confused. After all, he was only asking Fred about Daphne because *he* had feelings for Velma.

"Don't sweat the small stuff!" Fred said. "Summertime is fun time."

Fred reached into someone's golf bag and pulled out a club. Then he walked over and handed the club to a golfer in plaid shorts. Shaggy did the same. Gee, this caddy business wasn't too hard at all!

Back at the clubhouse, Scooby had an even easier time of it. He was sunning himself by an enormous pool and enjoying the dog days of summer. Daphne and Velma brought him a tasty tropical drink with a little paper umbrella in it.

At the golf clubhouse restaurant, the girls poured water into glasses and made sure the tables were ready for the lunch rush. There was a busy day of waiting tables ahead, but they were ready to roll!

But Daphne was a little distracted. She couldn't stop thinking about Fred — and the prospects for their summer romance.

"Of course, he's *totally* my boyfriend," Daphne explained to Velma.

"Hmmm, he is?" Velma said thoughtfully. "But I always thought football players liked to, er . . . play the field?"

"Me, too!" Daphne laughed. "I never thought Fred was looking for a serious relationship . . .

but he totally is! I just know it! He really is."

A pack of golfers moved into the club and asked to be seated for lunch. Velma and Daphne showed them to a large table and took their order. Another group came in after them. The lunch hour rush was on!

Before long, Fred and Shaggy came in off the links, exhausted. The girls were tired now, too. Oh, how their feet ached!

Everyone joined Scooby-Doo for some late-afternoon relaxing by the pool. Everyone collapsed onto chairs and ordered drinks in enormous cups with chunks of pineapple and twirly straws. The only thing Scooby had to show for his day was a totally radical sunburn.

"Velma?" Shaggy asked, his eyes lighting up. "Like, how was your day, Dinkley?"

"My day? Fine, I guess," she answered.

"My day was fine, too!" Shaggy cried. "Wow, isn't it crazy how much we have in common?"

"Huh?" Velma blinked at him.

Daphne had some big news for everyone. Uncle Thorny had extended a special invitation to the gang. They were invited to attend tonight's opening reception at the golf club! There would be a white tent pitched out on the property — and live music, too.

But Velma didn't look so interested. "I think I may pass on the reception," she explained. "Since we've arrived, I've been eager to survey the indigenous flora and fauna, so I think I'll check that out. . . ."

"No way! They have both flora *and* fauna up here?" Shaggy cried. "Like, wow! When was the last time you heard those two things mentioned in the same sentence?"

"Who knows?" Velma said. "See you guys later."

"Wait up, V!" Shaggy cried. He chased after her, followed by a very curious Scooby-Dooby-Doo.

"You know," Velma said, turning to Shaggy and Scooby as the three of them approached the banks of the lake. "I can't believe you'd pass up party snacks for a walk with me. I've never known you to be, well, intellectually curious."

"Aw, I'm curious about a lot of things, V," Shaggy said. "Like people. And relationships. And relationships *between* people."

Shaggy was trying to get Velma to talk about what was happening between them. But she didn't get it.

Scooby started to giggle. From behind Shaggy, he pulled out a violin and began to play romantic music.

But Velma didn't hear it. Her eyes had landed on something else; something sparkly in the muck.

"Jinkies!" Velma said. "I see something! I think it may be a rare moonstone!" She leaned toward the mud and reached for the stone. "Aha!" she cried as she held it up between her fingers.

The moonstone caught the moonlight and cast an eerie kaleidoscope of colors across Velma's face.

"Native Americans believed moonstones held a mystical connection with the moon. That's where the name comes from. Just look at how it glows. . . ." Velma said.

"It's almost as beautiful as your eyes," Shaggy said with a sigh.

"Oh, Shaggy . . ."

"Oh, Velma . . ."

"*Ooooooh*, Shaggy . . ."

"Roh, NO!" Scooby said. He poked a finger into his mouth like he was going to throw up. This was just too much — even for a dog!

But Velma wasn't being romantic. And she wasn't making eyes at anyone.

Velma Dinkley was about to get sick!

CHAPTER 4

"**U**m, Shaggy . . ." Velma said, clutching her stomach. "I think I bet**ter** find a place to lie down for a while. . . ."

She staggered off toward a large white reception tent that had been set up on the lawn. Uncle Thorny had spared no expense. Lights on the lawn glimmered pink and yellow and green. There was a faint sound of a band tuning up their instruments. It was the summer party at Erie Pointe Country Club — and it was just getting started.

Crowds of people strolled into the tent in their most stylish summer outfits.

But as Shaggy approached the tent, he felt sad. "Scoob, do you think Velma got sick . . . because of what I said?" he asked Scooby. "Did my *affections* make her sick?"

23

Scooby tried to listen, but he was distracted. He sniffed wildly at the air.

"Like, what's that smell?" Shaggy asked.

"BUFFET!" they yelled together.

The pair zipped across the lawn toward the big tent *and* (more importantly) toward the big food inside the big tent.

Just inside the entryway, Uncle Thorny was holding court. A distinguished-looking politician shook his hand.

"Hello, Senator," Uncle Thorny said. "I'm so glad you could make it."

"I wouldn't miss this party for the world," the senator said. "And I couldn't very well say 'no' to my biggest contributor, could I?"

Scooby poked Shaggy in the ribs. "Rurry up!" he yowled.

"Like, hold onto your fur. I'm hungry, too," Shaggy whispered back.

Daphne appeared with her arms crossed. "Excuse me, but where have you two been?" she asked. "And where's Velma?"

Velma? Shaggy had nearly forgotten!

He had to tell Daphne about how Velma had felt sick. He wanted to explain that maybe *he* had something to do with Velma feeling sick. But he didn't know where to begin. Besides, those itty-bitty cocktail franks in maple sauce and the grilled pepperoni pizza bites and the little flaky cheesy puffs were calling out to him from the buffet table across the tent.

Scooby was ready to eat, too. He grabbed a large white cloth napkin from the table edge and tucked it under his chin.

The two of them were about to stuff their mouths with the entire spread when a super-strong gust of wind blew into the tent. The canvas walls shuddered. A thick green fog started to fill in the gaps around the tent entrance. Within moments, the fog poured in. It was impossible to see anything — not even the food.

"Like, who ordered the pea soup?" Shaggy asked. "Anyone have a spoon?"

"Your attention, everyone!" Uncle Thorny announced. "There is a slight problem with the power generators . . ."

On one side of the white tent, a large, looming shadow appeared. Everyone saw it move.

"What is THAT!?" the guests inside the tent yelled.

It drew closer and closer. . . .

And got larger and larger. . . .

"Uh . . . F-F-Fred?" Daphne stammered. "What *is* that?"

"I don't know, Daph," Fred said matter-of-factly.

Shaggy's knees knocked. Scooby's teeth chattered.

"Please don't tell me you're thinking what I'm thinking?" Shaggy asked Scooby.

"Rake Ronster?" Scooby responded nervously.

"I said *don't* tell me!" Shaggy cried.

With a loud *rrrrrrip*, the tent wall shredded apart. Standing there in the darkness of the party was the real, live Lake Monster of Erie Pointe!

"Excuse me," Uncle Thorny told the enormous creature. "I don't recall sending *you* an invitation—"

The monster's huge tongue darted out of its mouth. It wrapped around Uncle Thorny and tossed him up into the air. Thorny flew onto a table with a loud crash.

"Like, *RUUUUUUUUN*!" Shaggy wailed.

Party guests ran in every direction. Everyone screamed and tripped over one another. Scooby dove into a punch bowl. Daphne, Fred, and Shaggy ducked behind the buffet table.

All the commotion made the Lake Monster madder! It charged back around the tent with full force and whipped its tail around the room again. A few people got knocked right over!

"This thing can't be real, can it?" Fred asked.

"I don't want to get close enough to find out," Daphne said.

One table flew into the air, and Fred came face-to-face with the beast. He raised a chair and cracked the monster on the head. *Crash!*

The Lake Monster barely flinched.

Crack!

The monster stumbled. It bumped into a tent post.

But that turned out to be disastrous! The tent began to collapse on itself. Everyone screamed. The guests were all covered — and trapped — by the heavy canvas fabric.

The monster turned and slinked back toward the lake.

"He's getting away!" Daphne said.

Fred and Uncle Thorny rushed to help lift up the tent canvas.

"Like, I knew we should have taken those summer jobs at Mustard Hut!" Shaggy cried.

By now, almost all the party guests were gone — or going. It didn't take long for Uncle Thorny to get the power on, but the guests weren't coming back! People wouldn't stay at Erie Pointe with a Lake Monster on the loose.

"Oh, dear," Uncle Thorny sighed. "I'm sure there's a logical explanation for this! We'll get the tent back up and get the golf course fixed up. We can get our guests back, can't we? We can put out some more food on the buffet. . . ."

Scooby's ears perked up.

"Did he say more food?" Shaggy whispered.

"Shaggy! Scooby!" Daphne said. "How can you think of eating at a time like this?"

The senator took off, too. "Sorry, Thorny," she said as she walked out. "Your problems make health care look easy."

All at once, Velma appeared at the edge of the destroyed tent.

"*Velma!*" Daphne cried. "You're safe!"

Velma scratched her head as she looked around at the mess and the chaos and all the people walking out. "Why do I get the distinct feeling that I missed something significant here?"

"It was the Lake Monster, V!" Shaggy wailed. "The Lake Monster of Erie Pointe was *here*. And it was the most terrifying, most scary thing ever!"

"The Lake Monster?" Velma rubbed her eyes. "Are you serious, Shaggy?"

"Oh, this is very serious," Uncle Thorny moaned. "Most of my guests will probably cancel their memberships — and it's only the first day we've been open. Did you see what that lake *thing* did to my property!? My golf course is supposed to be an eighteen-hole course. Now it looks like a hundred and eighteen holes! This is going to be a very short summer for all of us!"

Daphne threw her arms around her uncle. "Don't despair, Uncle T!" she said. "We need these jobs. We have to help you save Erie Pointe!"

"How can you kids save my place?" Uncle Thorny said.

Velma's face broke into a wide smile. "Aha!" she said to Fred, Daphne, and Shaggy. "Are you thinking what *I'm* thinking?"

Fred and Daphne nodded.

"Like, no way!" Shaggy said, waving his hands in their faces. "Not again . . ."

"Uncle Thorny," Daphne interrupted. "We have something to tell you. You didn't just hire summer help when you hired us. You hired the finest supernatural detectives in the tri-state area!"

"Huh?" Uncle Thorny looked completely baffled. "I *did*?"

"You betcha!" Velma snapped her fingers in the air. "And we know exactly how to start this investigation!"

CHAPTER

Velma pulled out the travel brochure that she had been reading at Trowburg's Gas and Goods. She held up the blurry photo of the Lake Monster.

"Let's start our investigation with Elmer Uggins! He's the guy who took the only known photograph of the Lake Monster of Erie Pointe. He has to know something," Velma said.

In the brochure there was a photo of Uggins. He had salt-and-pepper colored hair. In his hand was an old-fashioned camera. The caption said, Erie Pointe Lighthouse Keeper.

So Uggins lived in the old lighthouse on Erie Pointe! Even though it was late at night, the gang raced off to find him.

"I think it's a little strange — and convenient — that our first suspect just happens to be the keeper of a spooky lighthouse," Fred said.

"Like, just once I wish we could find a mystery that started in a cheery futon showroom!" Shaggy said.

"Huh?" Velma said.

"Why not?" Shaggy said. "Futons offer far more support than traditional mattresses."

The gang approached the doorway of the lighthouse. Daphne rang the doorbell.

WOOOOOOOOOOOOOOHOOOOOOOOOO.

The bell sounded like a foghorn. Shaggy nearly leaped out of his own skin.

"Well, the lights *are* on," Velma observed, looking around.

"But nobody's home," Fred finished.

Shaggy brightened up. "Hey, isn't this the part of our mystery where we split up and search for clues? Uh . . . I think I'll go with Velma!"

Shaggy smiled at Velma. His eyes twinkled. Without missing a beat, he grabbed her hand and dragged her off to look for clues.

"What was *that* about?" Fred asked. "Aw, never mind. Let's go, Daph." Scooby bounded after them.

Velma wrestled free from Shaggy's grip. They began their search of the grounds of the lighthouse keeper's residence.

As they were walking around, Shaggy leaned in close to Velma and sniffed. "Velma, what *is* that sweet, sweet fragrance you're wearing?"

"Bug and tick repellent," Velma said.

Shaggy sniffed more deeply. "Well, it's not repelling me! Isn't this a lovely night?"

"I guess," Velma said, pushing her glasses up her nose.

"I've always enjoyed walking beneath the full moon, minus the werewolves, of course. . . ."

"I don't mind walking by the light of the silvery moon, either . . ." Velma added.

Shaggy recognized that line from a song he'd heard once or twice before. He began to hum. As he looked at Velma, the moonlight danced across the top of her head. A dreamy look came over his face.

Shaggy started to daydream. In the dream, his surfer shorts turned into pants, and he sported a red-and-white striped vest and a straw hat. Velma was dressed up, too, as if they'd been transported back into time. Back to the 1900s!

"By the light . . . of the silvery *mooooooon*," Shaggy sang.

Velma grinned up at him, blinking. Was she *flirting*? In Shaggy's dream, anything was possible.

"I want to *grooooooove* . . ." Shaggy went on, singing. "To my honey I'll croon love's tune. . . ."

Daphne, Fred, and Scooby appeared out of

Meet the kids from Mystery, Inc.
—Daphne, Fred, Shaggy, Velma,
and Scooby-Doo.

The gang's got a mystery to solve — and as usual, Scooby and Shaggy want nothing to do with it.

But for Daphne, Fred, and Velma, this case is business as usual.

Shaggy's got something besides food at stake this time around — new feelings for his old friend Velma.

But Velma's too focused on the case to take much notice.

The case of the Lake Monster teaches the gang one thing: If they're going to solve mysteries, they've got to do it together.

nowhere. They were singing, too! Everyone, dressed for a barbershop quartet.

"Honeymoon! Keep a-shinin' in June . . . your silvery beams will bring love's dreams . . ."

The tune switched to funk, and Scooby was a deejay at a sound booth, scratching out a cool beat. Shaggy and Velma danced together in slow motion, looking deep into each other's eyes. The light danced all around.

But then Shaggy realized that they were still at the lighthouse of Erie Pointe, not in a dance club. There was no deejay. It was just him and Velma.

Sigh.

The light circled past him and Velma. Then it got dark. Then the light came back around. And there was something in the light!

"Did you see that?" Shaggy asked Velma. Velma cleared her throat nervously. "Did you surmise that it was a heretofore unclassified amphibious humanoid?"

"Uh, actually, I thought it was —"

Just then, the light stopped on a familiar, massive, froglike shape.

"*LAKE MONSTER! ZOINKS! RUUUUN!*"

Velma and Shaggy sped down the rocks, running away from the Lake Monster as fast as their feet would take them.

* * *

On the other side of the lighthouse, Daphne and Fred continued their own investigation. Scooby was sniffing around for snacks . . . er, clues, too.

"Hey, Daph," Fred asked quietly. "You don't think that Shaggy has some kind of crush on Velma, do you? I mean, he was asking me a lot of questions, and I tried to give him some advice, but . . ."

"Oh?" Daphne cracked a smile. "Exactly what kind of advice have you been giving Shaggy on dating?"

"Not much," Fred said. "Just that it's summer-time and he should try to have fun. . . ."

"*Aaaaaaaaaaaaaaaaaaaaaaaaah!*"

There was a loud scream from the darkness. It sounded just like Shaggy and Velma.

"Ruh-roh!" Scooby cried.

Shaggy and Velma were still being chased by the Lake Monster!

And they were coming this way!

CHAPTER

"**W**atch out!" Shaggy wailed as he saw Daphne, Fred, and Scooby. "The Lake Monster is chasing—"

"*Yowwwwwww!*" The monster cried out as it tripped on a giant rock and landed with a thud. "My ankle!"

"Huh?" Fred raced over to the monster. "It talked?"

Right away, the gang could tell that this was no monster. It was nothing but a man in a costume.

Fred lifted off the head.

"Mr. Uggins?!" Daphne exclaimed.

Fred helped the man up to his feet.

"Aw, call me Elmer," Uggins mumbled. "I can explain everything."

The gang gathered around Elmer Uggins's kitchen table to hear his explanation.

Elmer told the gang that he wanted to make a quick buck, so he'd *staged* the photograph of the Lake Monster of Erie Pointe. He'd used this costume.

"I took the pic, made some postcards of the fuzzy image, and sold 'em. It kept the tourist traps happy. People were visiting Erie Pointe from all over," Uggins explained. "After I heard about all the hoopla at the country club tonight, I figured I had a chance to scare some new tourists. I took out old green-eyes here and had some fun."

He held up the Lake Monster costume. Up close, it looked more droopy than scary.

"Great," Daphne said. "The creepy lighthouse keeper *didn't* do it. So now what?"

"Well, if the monster's a fake . . ." Fred sighed.

"Like, hold onto your hero sandwich! That monster at the tent was *not* fake," Shaggy said.

"He did look real," Daphne said.

"Reah, reah!" Scooby said. "Really real!"

"Well," Uggins said. "I never said the actual Lake Monster was a fake. I just said the photo was a fake."

"But how can the Lake Monster possibly be real?" Fred argued. "You know what? I bet it's probably just some prankster with a better costume."

"Maybe," Uggins said. "But there's a long history here. Want to hear it?"

Elmer Uggins lifted a can of coffee from the shelf. He poured himself a cup and offered the gang some.

"The legend of the Lake Monster goes way back, kids," Uggins started to explain, slurping his coffee. "Goes back before my time even, to the very beginnings of the town."

"Tell us the whole story," Fred said. "Don't leave anything out."

"Very well," Uggins said. "The story of Erie Pointe's Lake Monster goes back to when the first settlers arrived in these parts. They were confronted by an old woman who lived in a cave by the lake."

"Rave? Ry the rake?" Scooby's teeth chattered loudly.

Uggins's brows creased. "The lake woman's name was Grubwort. Wanda Grubwort. She claimed all the land around the lake belonged to her. And she said if the settlers didn't give it back, they'd be sorry."

He pulled a book off his dusty shelf and flipped it open to a picture of Wanda Grubwort. Well, it was a color drawing, not a photo. But it was the image of a witchy-looking old woman in a tattered cloak. Under the picture was a nameplate: WANDA GRUBWORT. In her hand was a gnarled branch covered with glowing stones, with a crown of stones at the very top. The staff was raised high over Wanda's head, and a beam of blue light was shooting out of it. Was she casting some kind of spell on Erie Pointe Lake? That's what it looked like!

"Wanda used her magical staff to transform an innocent lake creature into a hideous beast," Uggins went on. "And once she had the monstrous slave, she set it upon the villagers of Erie Pointe. Or at least that's what the legend claims."

"Like, she made good on her promise to wreak revenge, didn't she?" Shaggy said.

"Those villagers must have been really sorry," Daphne added. "What an awful fate!"

"What's *really* awful," Velma said, "is that this page in the book says the villagers burned Wanda the witch at the stake!"

"Roah!" Scooby gasped. "Rurn, raby, rurn?"

"I think you kids might want to think twice about staying here," Uggins said again. "The legend is true, I'm sure of it. Leave now while you still can."

"I'm sorry, Mr. Uggins. We just don't give up that easily," Fred said.

"Obviously you weren't in my sophomore geometry class," Shaggy said.

"Be careful, kids," Uggins said. "You've been warned."

The gang thanked Elmer Uggins and said good-bye.

On the walk back to the Mystery Machine, Shaggy and Scooby clung together like dryer sheets. Wanda Grubwort's curse sounded so terrible. The last thing the gang needed was another unexpected encounter with that Lake Monster — or worse.

They needed a better plan to destroy the monster, help Uncle Thorny, and save their summer jobs. Otherwise there would be no cash to pay back Old Man Frickert!

Fred powered up the Mystery Machine and headed back to the Erie Pointe Country Club. A decent night's sleep would do them all a lot of good.

But on the way out of the car, Shaggy heard a funny noise.

"What was that?" he yelped.

Daphne and Fred looked up for the source of the noise.

Click. Click. Click.

A security camera was following their every move!

Shaggy didn't mind that a camera was snapping pics of him. What a showoff! He and Scooby twirled around and struck a pose, waiting for the camera to snap.

"Nice moves, Twinkletoes!" Daphne said. "You like your photo ops, huh?"

"Like, whoa! That's it!" Shaggy stopped short in the middle of his pose. "I bet that monster had *its* own photo op!"

"A real roto rinish?" Scooby said.

"Yes! We should ask Uncle Thorny to show us the security cameras right away," Velma cried. "That footage may give us our first big clue to the identity of our Lake Monster . . . and whatever else is lurking at Erie Pointe."

CHAPTER

The gang had a fitful night's sleep. In just one short day, the country club had turned into a real haunted hideout. Uncle Thorny had his hands full!

Everyone woke up the next morning with a long list of work to do. They needed to keep their minds off the Lake Monster and help Thorny at the same time.

Daphne and Velma got to work setting up tables at the Erie Pointe Country Club Café. Shaggy was supposed to help Fred on the golf links, but he got distracted by the warmed-up rolls and butter at the café. At one point, he grabbed a few napkins and stuffed those into his mouth, too.

"What are you eating now?" Daphne asked.

"Doctor says I need more linen in my diet," Shaggy said.

"Oh, brother! Where's Fred?" Daphne asked.

"Golf course," Shaggy said. "I should get back there, too."

All Fred seemed to be doing was puttering around. And he wasn't puttering alone on the green. A few cute girls in golf skirts were there, too!

As soon as she saw the girls, Daphne's eyes widened — and then quickly narrowed.

"Fred!" Daphne barked.

Fred gulped when he heard Daphne's voice. He quickly shooed the golf girls away. "What's up, Daph?" Fred asked. "Shaggy, where did *you* go?"

"Shaggy, stay out of it," Daphne said.

"Actually," Shaggy said. "I really need to talk to you for a minute."

"This isn't the best time," Daphne growled.

"Why not?" Fred said. "Go ahead, Shag."

Shaggy cleared his throat nervously. "Well, I have this friend with a goatee, well, no, he doesn't actually have a goatee, that would be too obvious. Anyway he sort of likes this other friend. And he's not really sure; I mean, my friend without the goatee isn't really sure what to do about the fact that he's sort of in like with this . . ."

"Shaggy, we already know you like Velma," Fred said matter-of-factly.

"Like, what?" Shaggy said. "What are you talking about?!"

Scooby rolled his eyes.

"We know," Daphne said. "So is that all you wanted to say?"

"I just don't know what you're all talking about!" Shaggy said.

Just then Velma appeared, waving her arms at the rest of the gang. She'd gotten access to the video footage from the security cameras; now she needed everyone to come take a look.

"You're not going to believe what I saw on this film!" Velma announced. "After you watch this, you'll *all* be saying 'Jinkies!'"

The gang quickly followed Velma into the Erie Pointe Security Room. It was really dark. Scooby and Shaggy wrapped themselves together. After all, a scary monster might show up at any moment.

Velma clicked the PLAY button, and the footage began to roll. It showed the party in the moments immediately before the lake monster's attack.

"Wow! The security cameras caught the attack!" Daphne said.

"They caught the exact moment when the tent collapsed!" Shaggy said.

"Yeah, and they caught something else, too. . . ." Velma said.

She clicked a few buttons, and the screen showed a different scene. Now the footage showed a perspective along the shoreline. There was a Lake Monster right in the shot — but there was another cloaked figure there, too!

"*Two* pranksters, see?" Velma said.

"JINKIES!" everyone said at the same time.

Velma smiled. "Told ya."

The hooded figure started to turn toward the camera. It was hard to see a face.

"Freeze that frame!" Fred yelled.

Velma hit FREEZE, but the button stuck. She clicked another button to zoom in close on the cloaked figure's face, but then the computer went *ZZZZZAP!*

"Oh, no! What happened?" Fred cried.

"Like, that spooky figure must be using some kind of creepy magic to prevent us from seeing its face!" Shaggy said.

"I'm afraid the explanation is less supernatural than that," Velma said, pointing down to the desk. "I spilled my cup of water. It short-circuited the hard drive."

The computer went *ZZZZZZT* again. It really was fried.

"I understand this is a great disappointment," Velma said. "I'll tender my resignation from the group immediately. . . ."

"Like, hold on just a minute, Velma!" Shaggy said. "Don't beat yourself up about making this mistake. You just pulled a Shaggy, okay?"

"Reee-heeee!" Scooby snickered. "Rulled a Raggy! Rhat's runny!"

Velma just shook her head. "There's no excuse for why that happened. It's so unlike me."

She wandered off sadly. The gang let her go.

"She'll be okay," Daphne said. "Shaggy, you obviously do have feelings for Velma."

"Like, what do you mean by that?" Shaggy said. But then he threw his arms up into the air. "Okay, fine," he sighed. "I give up. I admit it. I like Velma. I like my friend!"

"You know, I can help you out with that," Fred said. "I know all about girls. . . ."

"Oh you do?" Daphne said, crossing her arms. "Like those girls on the golf course?"

"Uh . . ." Fred stammered. "About those girls . . ."

"Look, I think I'll leave you two alone now," Shaggy said. "I'll just figure it out myself. I want my relationship to be the real deal. Not some loosey-goosey thing like you two have anyway!" Shaggy strode out of the room, with Scooby behind him. As soon as they were gone, Daphne turned to Fred with a look of accusation.

"What did he mean by 'loosey-goosey'? What

have you been telling everyone about us?" Daphne asked.

"Nothing," Fred said. "I mean, I just explained how our relationship is casual, a real summer thing . . ."

"Oh, casual? Is that so?" Daphne said.

"I mean, we're just hanging out, right?" Fred asked uncertainly. "Casual."

"Oh, yeah. Totally. Casual. Yes, I'm so glad we want the exact same thing," Daphne said, supersarcastically, before punching Fred in the arm — hard.

Fred scratched his head as she walked away. "I will never in a zillion years understand girls."

From just behind where Fred stood, the bushes rustled. A cloaked figure moved into view, and then back into the shadows again.

Fred was so distracted, he didn't notice. Neither did any of the others.

But the cloaked figure was there.

And it was watching them!

CHAPTER

"**R**aggy, ret's ret a ridnight rack!" Scooby grumbled. "Ri'm rungry! Row about a rew randwiches?"

"I can't eat," Shaggy moaned.

Scooby's ears perked up. "Rhat!?" He leaned in and felt Shaggy's forehead with his paw. "Rhat's the ratter rith roo?"

"Like, I was just practicing in front of the mirror," Shaggy explained. "I was practicing what to say to Velma. Because, buddy, I do like her. And I want to tell her but I don't know when . . . or how."

Scooby moaned. "*Noooooooooooo!* Rhelma?" He lifted his paws and felt his own doggy forehead.

All around them, the fog was getting thick again, just like the night before. Shaggy pulled his hoodie around himself and shivered.

"What do I do now, Scoob?"

"Rorget Rhelma!" Scooby said. "Ret's reat!"

Shaggy just shook his head. The two of them wandered off in search of the nearest kitchen. Maybe a little ketchup, mayo, mustard, and marshmallow spread on a human-sized bread wedge would do the trick.

* * *

On the other side of the Erie Pointe Country Club, Fred was out for a walk when he noticed the fog starting to roll in. He needed to find Daphne and make sure she was okay.

But what he found was Daphne on the tennis court . . . playing tennis with three teen boys! They were in the middle of a night-owl tennis match. The bright lights cut through some of the foggy night.

"Daphne!" Fred called out when he saw her.

"Oh, Fred," Daphne said, twirling her tennis racquet. "It's you. Something wrong?"

"What are you doing here?" Fred asked.

Daphne smiled. "Playing around."

Fred scowled. He grabbed Daphne by the hand and dragged her down the path off the tennis court. By now, the fog was really rolling in and it was getting hard to see, even with all those lights.

Daphne waved good-bye to her tennis triplets. Fred scowled again.

On the way, the pair ran into Shaggy, who looked terrified! They thought it was just the fog spooking him.

But Shaggy explained that he was feeling bad about something other than fog.

"I think I smell Eau de Dinkley," Shaggy sighed.

"Eau de wha?"

Shaggy sniffed the air like Scooby usually did. "Velma's out here. I know it. Velma! Velma!"

Unfortunately the mist was so thick, it was impossible to see anything. But Shaggy, Daphne, and Fred glimpsed something moving a short distance away.

They all yelled out at the same time.

"VELMA!!!!"

"Raaaaaaaaaaaaaaaargh!"

They stopped short. That wasn't Velma! Not even close.

THAT was the Lake Monster!

"Help!" Shaggy cried. "Run away! Run away!"

He took off on foot with the monster at his

heels. But the monster was moving in circles. In no time, Shaggy *and* the monster were right back where they started.

"Run, Fred!" Daphne cried as they approached. "The monster will get you! Run!"

"No way," Fred said. He planted his feet firmly on the ground. "I'm sick of this monster. Once and for all I'm going to unmask this prankster!"

First, Fred whipped a tennis racquet at the monster's head, but the monster reached out and deflected the racquet with ease. That made Fred angry. He went airborne. In one big swoop, he jumped and tackled the monster to the ground.

The two struggled to squirm free.

"Daphne! Shaggy! I need help!" Fred called out.

They came running. Everyone leaped onto the monster. Shaggy held it down. Daphne pulled on its jowls. Fred desperately tried to rip off its mask.

"*ROOOOOOOOOOAR!*" the monster howled in pain.

"Uh, Fred," Daphne said. "I don't think that's a mask. Maybe you better stop pulling on its—"

"*ROOOOOOOOOOAR!*" the monster howled again. This time, its mouth opened wider than ever, and a bunch of wriggling, wet, slimy fish popped out. Half an ocean's worth!

"Gross!" Daphne said, shutting her eyes.

They all jumped back.

"Something is *still* super-fishy about this monster," Shaggy said.

"Ya think so?" Daphne cracked.

The monster picked itself right up and started to give chase again. The gang took off in all directions. But for some reason, the monster kept chasing after Shaggy!

The Lake Monster bared its yellow fangs and moved in closer and closer until . . .

"Ri'll rave rou!" Scooby called out of the darkness. He leaped pawsfirst over one of the golf greens and right into the middle of that monster mash.

"Like, wow, Scoob!" Shaggy said. "I thought for sure that mutant frog was about to make me croak. You saved me."

"Rhat are riends ror?" Scooby snickered. He flexed his muscles proudly.

But the monster was still after them!

Its long, sticky tongue whipped out and nearly knocked over the two of them with one lick! Could this Lake Monster be stopped?

Shaggy and Scooby raced for cover. They revved up a nearby golf cart and started to motor away from the scene of the crime. If they could just distract the monster, then they might be able to catch it off guard, or at least escape and hide in a safer place.

But Shaggy was so busy worrying that he missed a turn on the course. The cart went flying into a sand trap!

"Zoooooooooooinks!"

Shaggy landed head first. When he came up for air, he had something in his hand. It was a shiny stone just like the one Velma had found the day before.

"Doesn't this look like one of those moon-stones?" Shaggy said. "Velma loves these things. Maybe I should keep it for her."

Shaggy shoved the stone into his pocket and wandered off to find his true love. Scooby hurried after him.

Fred and Daphne were still worried the Lake Monster might turn back for them.

"Is the coast clear?" Fred asked through the fog. "I still say there's no such thing as a Lake Monster. This is someone's no-good trick."

"Tell that to the monster. It just threw up an entire aquarium and then ran away!" Daphne cried.

All at once, there was a loud burping noise.

"Oh, no," Fred whispered.

And just like that, the Lake Monster appeared

again — directly in front of them! It looked madder than ever!

"CROOOOOOOOOOOOAK!"

"Look out!" Fred called. He saw the monster's tongue whip out. This time, it slurped Daphne's head.

"*Ewwww!*" Daphne moaned.

Fred grabbed a golf club and went after the beast. He took a few sharp swings at the monster's mutant frog feet.

"What are we going to do?" Daphne cried. "How can we get away from this thing? Mr. Lake Monster, do you think maybe you could find it in your heart to let us go. I mean, I really and truly love frogs and I think that—"

"ROOOOOOOOOOOOAR!"

"Nice one, Daph," Fred said. "That really did the trick."

Fred raised another golf club and slammed it down harder than before. That *did* do the trick. The monster yelped. It hopped up and down in pain.

Before the monster could recover, Fred and Daphne ducked for cover inside the Erie Pointe pro shop.

CHAPTER

If Fred and Daphne stood perfectly still, like mannequins, the monster would never be able to identify them, would he? The two teens grabbed some bright golf clothes along with a couple of wigs. They struck a pose.

It didn't take long before the monster crept into the shop, panting.

"Don't move a muscle," Fred whispered.

The Lake Monster's fishy breath was worse than ever! It hissed angrily when it couldn't find anyone to attack.

"CREATURE!"

Daphne and Fred froze in position. That was not the monster. It was another voice. Who else was here?

"What are you doing?" the second voice hissed louder. Another figure came into view. It wore a brown, tattered cloak, just like the one on the security camera footage.

Daphne wanted to scream. But she stayed perfectly still. So did Fred.

"With all the bedlam you've raised tonight," the cloaked figure hissed at the Lake Monster, "we'll have to stop early. Return to the lake now. I will summon you when it is safe to resume our search. . . ."

The Lake Monster slinked out of the shop.

Daphne's mind raced. What search was the figure talking about? How had it controlled the Lake Monster? Where did these creatures come from? And who was this cloaked figure, anyway?

As the figure in the cloak slipped away, Daphne noticed something on its back. That cloak was streaked with purple paint! She'd recognize that color anywhere!

They had uncovered a new clue!

"Let's go find Uncle Thorny and the others!" Fred said. "We haven't got much time."

As they shuffled back to the main clubhouse, Daphne noticed that Velma wasn't with the group.

"Velma?" she called out.

"Over here!" Fred responded. Velma was there, slumped on a rock.

Shaggy ran right over. *"VELMAAAAAA!"* He looked so worried. "Is she dead?" he sobbed.

Daphne leaned over and felt for Velma's pulse. Velma's eyes began to twitch.

"She's alive!" Shaggy howled.

Velma blinked and raised her head. She'd been knocked out for a little while. When the others asked what had happened, she couldn't recall at first. She said she'd gotten lost in the fog. She couldn't sleep so she'd gone for a walk by the lake. But when the fog rolled in, she got groggy and fell into dreamland.

"Don't ever do that again, do you hear me?!" Shaggy yelled at her. "We were worried sick . . . *eeeeeeeew!*"

Shaggy jumped back a little from Velma. She had mysterious black spots on her hand.

"What are *those?*" he asked.

"They kinda look like warts," Fred said.

"Oh, no," Velma said. "I'm sure it's just some kind of urushiol-induced dermatitis."

"Yeah, well, whatever it is," Fred said, "you missed a second Lake Monster attack. We have a lot to talk about!"

On the way to breakfast, Daphne reminded everyone about the paint splat she'd seen on the stranger's brown cloak. The purple paint splat!

"It was the same color as the boat we saw

down at the docks, don't you remember?" Daphne asked.

"Let's hit the docks then!" Fred said. He turned to walk away, and everyone followed.

Except Shaggy. He had an announcement to make before the group went anywhere.

"Excuse me, Velma!" he called out.

She turned around and smiled at him.

"Velma," Shaggy said, breathless. "I can wait no longer. I've been trying to do something since we got here. And life is a lot like the reception tent last night. If you wait too long, it'll collapse on you!" He dropped to his knees and reached for Velma's hand. "Velma, er . . . will you go on a date with me? Tonight?"

"A date?!" Velma exclaimed. "Shaggy, are you serious?!" She glanced nervously at Fred and Daphne. She didn't want Shaggy to feel badly. "That is so sweet, Shaggy," she began hesitantly. "But we're right in the middle of an investigation."

"Let's let Daphne and Fred take over the case. They probably want some more quality time together, anyway!" Shaggy said.

"Not really," Daphne said, shaking her head.

"Yeah, I'm good . . ." said Fred.

"I don't know, Shaggy," said Velma.

Shaggy hung his head. "Like, I understand. If I

were you, I wouldn't want to go out with a goofy guy like me either." He started to shuffle away.

Velma couldn't bear it. "Wait, Shaggy!" she called after him. "You know what? I will go out with you tonight."

"Ya mean it?" Shaggy cried.

"Sure! Why not?" Velma said.

* * *

That evening, Shaggy and Velma met up at the country club dining room for their "date." Velma was dressed in a ball gown that Daphne found in the closet of one of the rooms. She looked like she'd stepped back in time.

Shaggy was dressed up, too, in board shorts — and a bow tie.

The dining room was empty when they got there.

"Mm, strange . . ." Velma observed. "Perhaps we should check in with Daphne and Fred . . ."

"Hey, Velma, can you put those frontal lobes on the back burner please? Just for tonight?" Shaggy asked.

"Okay, Shaggy," Velma said. "I will try. I must confess, I haven't been feeling too much like myself lately."

Shaggy reached for a candle on the tabletop.

He lit a match and —

"*Aaaaaaaaaaaaaah!*" Velma recoiled and fell backward off her chair. Her eyeglasses flew off, too. Shaggy rushed over to help her up. He went to get her water. A waiter was right there, too, ready to pour some into the glass.

"Ranything relse?" the waiter said.

"SCOOBY!" Shaggy whispered angrily. He looked at Velma in a panic. But without her glasses, she didn't seem to notice their waiter was Scooby. So Shaggy picked up his fork and dropped it. "Uh, excuse me, Velma, I dropped my fork."

Shaggy pulled Scooby under the table for a little impromptu chat. "What are you doing here?"

"Ri'm raiting rables," Scooby said innocently.

"Get out of here, Scoob! You're going to ruin everything!"

"Ro!" said Scooby stubbornly.

"Scooby!" sighed Shaggy in frustration. Then he had an idea. "Would you do it for a Scooby Snack?"

Scooby folded his arms across his chest. "Ri ron't re rought!"

"Now listen, Scooby, I'm the master and I command you to go back to your room and stop being such a bad dog!" With that, Shaggy returned to Velma on the right side of the table again.

Scooby was fuming. "Rad rog? Rell . . . ri'll row rou a rad rog!"

"Did you find your fork?" Velma asked Shaggy.

"What? Oh, yes, I did, thanks — *YOWWW!*"

At that moment, Scooby flung himself at the table. Things went flying all over the place: Utensils, plates, and cups crashed around the room. Shaggy had a special gift for Velma, too, in his back pocket. Even that flew across the room and landed on the floor!

"What's *this?*" Velma said as she recovered it from the ground. It was the shard of moonstone. It glowed brightly as a moon.

"I found it on the golf course last night," Shaggy explained.

"It's *soooooo* beautiful . . ." Velma said. Her voice got dreamier than ever.

"I'm so glad you like it," Shaggy said.

"Okay. Gotta go," Velma announced abruptly. She turned on one heel. Before Shaggy could say another word, she was gone.

"Velma?" Shaggy called after her. *"Velma?"*

But she didn't hear him.

Shaggy turned to Scooby and wailed, *"This is all your fault!"*

CHAPTER

Daphne and Fred had work to do on the docks. They were ready to check out the purple paint clue — and solve the mystery of the cloaked figure by the lake.

"Look!" Daphne pointed to a sign near the purple boat. It read ERIE POINTE FLOATING MUSEUM.

"Ahoy!" Fred said as they walked aboard.

This was no ordinary museum. The walls of the boat were adorned with funny old portraits of ship captains and seafarers. There was art of the original Erie Pointe settlers, too, alongside mounted fish with wide eyes and gaping mouths. Shelves were crammed with old fishing poles and rusted harpoons.

"This place gives me the creeps," Daphne said.

"Hey, look!" Fred noticed something on the

floor of the museum. It was a set of footprints left in purple paint.

"Now *that* is a clue for sure!" Daphne said.

She and Fred began to follow the prints through the rest of the floating museum. They made their way into a small room marked ARCHIVES. That was the room where all the old records and photographs were stored.

The room was packed from floor to ceiling with steamer trunks and dusty boxes. Daphne noticed a trunk with the lock pried off. She flipped open the lid and found a mess of papers inside. She and Fred began to rifle through the box.

"Looks like old newspapers," Fred said.

Daphne found a paper with a familiar illustration on the front page. It was Wanda Grubwort and her evil staff!

"Read this," Daphne told Fred. "It's just like Elmer Uggins told us. Wanda Grubwort was burned at the stake. But check this out . . . her staff survived the fire!"

"That staff was the source of all her evil power," Fred said.

"Look at this headline!" Daphne said.

The headline read WITCH'S STAFF FINALLY DESTROYED. MAGIC STONES SCATTERED AND BURIED.

"Magic stones?" Fred asked.

"*That* must be what the Lake Monster wants

to get! The moonstones! They must be the source of Wanda's powers," Daphne concluded.

"But we still don't know who's controlling things," Fred said.

"Wait!" Daphne interjected. "Maybe we do! Here's an even better headline!"

ORPHANED CHILDREN OF WITCH FOUND IN CAVE! TOWNSPEOPLE TORN ON FATE!

"Wanda Grubwort had *children*?" Fred said. "She still may have descendants living in town."

"Maybe one of them got angry when Uncle Thorny built his place?" Daphne suggested. "And they wanted to seek revenge on my uncle — and anyone else involved in the place."

Fred and Daphne had found some terrific clues. Now they just had to figure out what to do next. But as they tried to exit the archives room, they found the door was stuck. No matter how hard they pulled, it wouldn't budge.

"If we don't get this open, we'll be here all night," Fred said.

Whooooooooooooooooooosh!

Without warning, water began to pour into the room. Now the locked door seemed like no problem at all compared to the impending flood of doom!

Daphne and Fred tried banging on the door. Water was filling the room fast.

Pretty soon, the water was all the way up to their waists.

"Do something, Fred!" Daphne yelped. "Before we drown!"

Fred tried again to push on the door. It still wouldn't budge.

"You know," Daphne went on, "if I'm going to die here, I don't want to die dating you!"

"Oh, really?" Fred groaned. "Well, take that—"

He tried to kick the door again.

"And that—"

CLUNK!

With the final thrust, the door to the archive room finally burst open and the water poured out of the room.

"I did it!" Fred cried.

"It doesn't change a thing." Daphne scowled. "We're still broken up."

The two of them ran from the purple-painted boat. They hurried off to the staff quarters to find everyone.

"Like, zoinks!" Shaggy exclaimed when they appeared back at the room — soaked to the bone. "What happened to you?"

"Fred and I broke up!" Daphne announced.

"No," Shaggy said. "What I meant was, 'Why are you all wet?'"

CHAPTER

11

Fred and Daphne filled everyone in on what had happened at the Erie Pointe Floating Museum, including what they'd read in the archive room about Wanda Grubwort and her long-lost ancestors.

"Hey!" Daphne said. She ran across the hotel room and found a beat-up copy of the town phone book. "Grubwort . . . Grubwort . . . let's see: Greene, Grimley . . . there's no Grubwort here!"

"Does she have another family name?" Fred asked.

"Hold it!" Shaggy cried out. "I just noticed something cool. What a crazy coincidence."

"What is it?" asked Fred.

"Remember when we first got to town, we stopped in at that creepy general store. It was called 'Trowburg's Gas and Goods,'" Shaggy explained. "And I just now realized that *Trowburg* spells *Grubwort* backward!"

Shaggy had seen the mirror reflection of the phone book. An advertisement for Trowburg's showed up "Grubwort" in the reflection.

"What are the odds, huh?" Shaggy asked.

"Everything's odd, if you ask me!" Daphne said, shaking her head.

"Hey, Shaggy," Fred asked. "What happened to Velma? Is she okay? Why isn't she here?"

Fred shrugged. "She's around here somewhere. Maybe she went back to the sleeping quarters. Or maybe she—"

"Is taking a nap on a rock somewhere again?" Daphne asked sarcastically.

"Hey! Like, that's my Velma you're talking about!" Shaggy cried.

Fred suggested that they all head over to the Trowburg residence to find Hilda Trowburg and ask a few more questions. They'd catch up with Velma later. The four friends hopped into the Mystery Machine and took off.

* * *

Once Fred, Daphne, Scooby, and Shaggy reached the spooky Trowburg house, they began to have a few doubts about their plan. A lightning strike outside lit up the place. Thunder sent shivers down Shaggy's spine. There, in the darkness of the house, the gang saw a cloaked figure walking through the halls.

"There she is!" Fred cried. "Okay, Shaggy and Scooby, you go around back and —"

"Unh-unh," said Shaggy, folding his arms across his chest. "I'm not going anywhere with him."

"Ritto," declared Scooby.

"Well, I'm not going anywhere with *him*," said Daphne, pointing at Fred.

A fight instantly broke out. "Forget it!" Fred cried at last. "Let's just all go together."

Quietly, the gang crept up the stairs of the house and through the front door.

All at once, the figure appeared again, walking quickly up and down the stairs.

"Ruh-roh," Scooby whimpered.

Fred, Daphne, Scooby, and Shaggy raced after the cloaked figure. After a few minutes of chase, Fred crept up behind the figure and wrestled him to the ground.

"At last!" Fred cried. "We can unmask the person behind this mystery!"

And with that, he pulled back the mask.

"NO WAY!" Daphne screeched.

Scooby's eyes popped clear out of his head.

"Like, it can't be!" Shaggy wailed. "It can't BE!"

But sure enough, the figure behind the mask was none other than . . .

Velma Dinkley!

CHAPTER

12

"**Y**ou fools!" Velma growled in a voice that definitely did not belong to her. *"I'm not Velma!"*

Everything that happened after that was a blur of smoke and light. Velma raised a large staff. It was covered with the moonstone pieces from all over the country club. Just as in the pictures they'd seen, there was a crown made of stones at the very top.

Velma waved the wand this way and that way.

"Velma," Fred barked. His fists were up. "I don't want to hurt you!"

"Ah, but I want to hurt *you*," Velma said in her creepy new voice.

"Like, why are you doing this?" Shaggy asked. "Our date wasn't that bad, was it?"

Velma raised the staff toward the sky again. As

she did, the moonstones began to glow brightly.

KA-BOOM!

All at once, the room exploded with a blue light.

* * *

A little while later, the gang woke up to find themselves in a smoky room inside the Trowburg residence. They felt a little groggy.

"Why is Velma doing this?" Daphne asked.

"You don't think my *love* drove Velma mad, do you?" Shaggy asked with concern.

Everyone laughed.

"I think there's something bigger than that going on, Shags," Fred said.

"I warned you!" a voice called out from under the staircase.

The gang huddled together. *What was that?*

And then Hilda Trowburg appeared, rubbing her eyes.

"Your friend has been possessed by the spirit of the evil Wanda Grubwort!" she cried.

"Great!" Shaggy sighed. "My very first love, and she's turned into a witch!"

Hilda explained to everyone how Velma must have located the stones to give the staff back its powers.

"You don't think moonstones had anything to do with this, do you?" Shaggy asked.

Hilda nodded. "As soon as your friend put those cursed rocks into the staff, my evil ancestor took over!"

The cloaked figure the gang had been following all over Erie Pointe was Velma Dinkley — the whole time!

Shaggy figured out that each time Velma found one of the stones, she acted a little stranger. She found a stone by the lake, then she got black warts on her hand. And she'd jumped when Shaggy lit the match for the candle.

"Like, I'd be freaked out by fire, too, if I'd been burned at the stake!" Shaggy said.

"I bet she made the security camera footage short-circuit on purpose," Daphne said. "Because she knew it would have shown *her* face!"

The gang looked at one another.

"How did we miss all those important clues?" Fred asked.

Daphne shrugged. "We were all so busy worrying about our own silly little relationships that we forgot to pay attention to the important signs!"

"There's one thing I don't understand," Shaggy said. "Why did Velma come back here tonight if she'd already found all the stones for her staff?"

"Ah," Hilda said. "But she had not found them all. There was one more. I had it here."

Hilda held out a now-empty box.

"I'm sorry I was unable to keep this final stone safe. Now Wanda Grubwort is getting ready for her ultimate revenge!"

"I don't care about Wanda!" Shaggy said. "I want to save Velma!"

"Where could she be hiding now?" Fred asked.

"The caves!" Hilda snapped her fingers. "I bet she went back to the place where she used to hide out from everyone else."

There was only one problem with finding Grubwort in the caves.

They were all underwater!

CHAPTER

The gang got decked out with flippers, tanks, and masks. As luck would have it, Hilda Trowburg rented scuba gear! Fred, Daphne, Shaggy, and Scooby swam quickly through the murky waters of Erie Lake in search of the cave entrances.

Scooby had his underwater camera with him so he could snap some photos of fish — and whatever else they might find under the sea.

It didn't take long to find the entrance to the caves. The group surfaced and climbed out of the water. They had to be very sneaky.

Quietly, they crept along the inside of one of the underwater caverns.

Velma was here! She and the Lake Monster were standing together at the back of one cave.

"You've been a faithful servant," Velma told the

monster. "I think you deserve a few playmates. . . ."

Velma waved her staff over the water. It rippled and bubbled. Within moments, three more glowing lake monsters rose up out of the water.

"She's making more of those things!" Fred said.

"Rise, my slithering slaves," Velma chanted. "Rise and greet your new master."

All of the new Lake Monsters roared with delight.

The gang had to act fast. The spirit of Wanda Grubwort was ready to seek revenge on all of Erie Pointe. She was making an army of Lake Monsters to take back the land she believed had been stolen from her.

There was only one thing they could do.

"VELMA, STOP!" Shaggy yelled, bursting out of his hiding spot.

"I told you, Velma doesn't live here anymore!" she hissed. Then she turned to her Lake Monsters and ordered them to attack.

"Shaggy?" Fred cried. "*That* was your plan?"

"No, no! Trust me!" Shaggy said. "I have an idea."

The Lake Monsters moved in on the gang, but Scooby raised his underwater camera and hit the

FLASH button. The monsters were blinded by the bright light.

"Velma!" Shaggy ran to her side again. "I know you're still in there! I know you can hear me!"

Velma sneered and raised her staff.

"Then again," Shaggy groaned. "Maybe you *can't* hear me. . . ."

But Shaggy wouldn't give up.

"LISTEN TO ME!" he pleaded. "You're stronger than this thing inside of you. You're stronger and you're smarter and you're . . . you're *cute*! That's right! I think you're cute!"

All at once, Velma blinked. "Shaggy, is that *you*?"

"Yes! It's me! You have to push this evil spirit out of you, Velma!"

But winning this battle was harder than Shaggy thought. Velma lifted her staff into the air and shot out a sizzling blue beam of light at him, pinning him to the cave wall.

On the other side of the underwater cavern, the Lake Monsters were chasing Fred and Daphne. The two teens thought they'd escaped, until they hit a stone wall. Dead end!

Fred turned to Daphne. "I'm sorry, Daph. I *was* a jerk."

"I'm sorry, too," Daphne said. "I should've

talked to you, told you how I felt, instead of trying to make you feel jealous."

They hugged for a moment, then turned in terror. They could hear the slimy footsteps of the Lake Monsters growing closer and closer. . . .

Meanwhile, Shaggy was determined to think of something to distract Wanda and get Velma back.

"I won't let a couple of moonstones ruin my — hey, that's it — MOON!"

Shaggy started to hum. "By the light of the silvery moon . . ."

It was the song he and Velma had sung together just a short time ago.

"Those silvery beams will bring love's dreams and we'll be cuddlin' soon . . ."

"That's . . . my . . . favorite . . . verse," panted Velma, struggling with Wanda's spirit. The song gave her a new reserve of strength. She could fight this evil spirit!

"GET OUT OF ME, WANDA GRUBWORT!" Velma shouted. She yanked the crown off the staff and flung it into the air.

There was a blinding flash of light, and the spirit of Wanda Grubwort rose out of Velma. The witch's spirit hovered ghostlike in midair. "Ha! Nothing's going to stop me now!" Wanda's spirit cackled.

"Rot ro rast!" cried Scooby. He leaped up, grabbed the crown, and threw it against the wall. It shattered into bits. "Ray rood-rye, ricked ritch!"

"*NO!*" Wanda cried. "REVENGE! REVENGE WAS IN MY GRASP!"

Fortunately for everyone, revenge was not to be. The evil spirit of Wanda Grubwort faded into nothingness.

"I would have gotten away with my plan, too," Wanda wailed as she disappeared, "if it wasn't for you meddling kids!"

And just like that — *poof!* — Wanda was gone for good.

Back at the dead end, Fred and Daphne were bracing themselves for another Lake Monster attack. They closed their eyes and huddled together. Until . . .

Ribbit! Fred carefully opened one eye. The Lake Monsters had returned to their true form: little green frogs!

"What happened?" Daphne asked in wonder. "Where did they go?"

"He did it! Shaggy did it!" Fred cheered. Without Wanda's power, the monsters' power could not survive. "Come on!"

CHAPTER

Back at the entrance to the cavern, Velma blinked and looked around. "Is it over? Is it really over?"

"Yeah, I think so," said Shaggy.

"Those things you said . . . did you really mean them?" Velma asked.

"Of course I did!" said Shaggy.

He stared deeply into Velma's eyes. She stared right back into his.

"Oh, just kiss her already!" Daphne cried as she and Fred rejoined their friends.

Velma and Scooby smiled at each other . . . and smooched. But . . .

"Let's try that again," said Shaggy awkwardly.

So they did.

When it was over, Shaggy said, "Wow, that was, uh . . ."

"Yeah," said Velma.

"I don't know too much about chemistry, but . . ." Shaggy began.

"Well, I do, and there wasn't any," Velma finished.

"Maybe we're just better off as friends," Shaggy said.

Velma nodded.

Fred and Daphne looked at each other.

"You know what?" Daphne said. "Maybe we all are."

* * *

That afternoon, the gang took all the pieces of staff and stones and placed them into dozens of separate envelopes. The envelopes were sent all over the world!

"They scattered the pieces around town last time. I bet scattering them across the globe will keep Wanda from coming back to life," Fred said.

Uncle Thorny hugged his niece. He had good news, too: Applications for the country club were already up. Business was booming again.

"Well, kids," Uncle Thorny went on, "I have a little something here to show my appreciation. . . ."

He produced a giant check for the amount of

ten thousand dollars! The "Payable to" line was blank.

"I didn't know how to spell Old Man Frickert," Thorny explained.

Daphne and Velma laughed. They'd helped Uncle Thorny get his work back on track. And it paid off — big time — for everyone.

"Our debt to Frickert is gone!" Fred said, "Now it's time to enjoy the rest of our summer!"

"I'd say it's also time for a Scooby Snack, wouldn't you, Scoob?" Shaggy asked.

Scooby nodded eagerly. "Rooby-rooby-roo!"